Halloween Hustle

by Charlotte Gunnufson

illustrated by **Kevan J. Atteberry**

Skeleton

two lions

For my family, Scott, Perry, Isaac, and Ellen
—C. G.

For my dear friends, Tom and Sue,
who have put me back together more than once
—K. J. A.

two lions

Text copyright © 2013 by Charlotte Gunnufson
Illustrations copyright © 2013 by Kevan J. Atteberry

Amazon Publishing
Attn: Amazon Children's Publishing
P.O. Box 400818
Las Vegas, NV 89140
www.amazon.com/amazonchildrenspublishing

Library of Congress Cataloging-in-Publication Data is available upon request.
ISBN-13: 9781477817230 (hardcover)
ISBN-10: 1477817239 (hardcover)
ISBN-13: 9781477867235 (eBook)
ISBN-10: 1477867236 (eBook)

The illustrations are rendered digitally in Photoshop.
Book design by Vera Soki
Editor: Marilyn Brigham

Printed in China (R)
First edition
10 9 8 7 6 5 4 3 2 1

In the dark, a funky beat.
Something white with bony feet.
Skeleton dancing up the street,
Doing the Halloween Hustle.

Bony thumbs and fingers snap.
Bony heels and toes tip-tap.
Knees knock-knock and elbows flap,
Doing the Halloween Hustle.

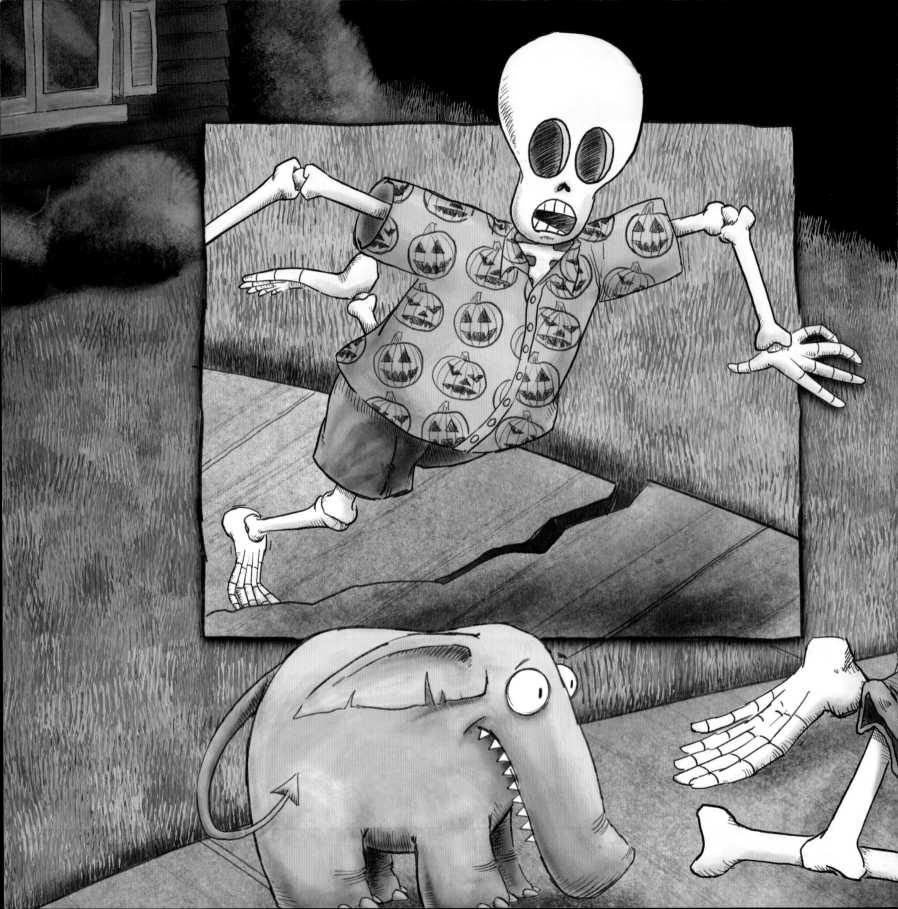

Skeleton twists his skinny hips.
Shakes his shoulders, skates and skips.
On a crooked crack, he trips . . .

Bones scatter!
What a clatter!
Spine is like a broken ladder!

He sticks his bones back into place,
Adds rubber bands, just in case.
Gets up and grooves with ghoulish grace,
Doing the Halloween Hustle.

He swings around the bus stop sign—
Once, twice—then gets in line
Right behind Frankenstein,
Doing the Halloween Hustle.

Climbs on the bus. Can't find a seat.
That's okay! He finds the beat.
Shuffles and scuffles those bony feet,
Doing the Halloween Hustle.

The big bus zigzags through the town.
Zooms up hills, then cruises down.
Every monster for miles around
Is doing the Halloween Hustle!

The bus slows down and then it stops.
Skeleton leaves with three high hops.
Leads the others to the shops,
Doing the Halloween Hustle.

Skeleton buys a snazzy hat,
A jazzy jacket to go with that.
But in his path, a big black cat . . .

Bones scatter!
What a clatter!
Spine is like a broken ladder!

Skeleton doesn't groan or whine.
Binds his bones with tape and twine.
He bounces up, feeling fine,
Doing the Halloween Hustle.

In fancy clothes, the monsters go
To the party in a row—
A funky, freaky fashion show!
Doing the Halloween Hustle.

The ghostly host greets each guest,
"How do you do? You're so well dressed!
Just in time for the dance contest,
Doing the Halloween Hustle!"

Monsters move on through the door.
Jump and jive out on the floor.
Spooky judges hold up scores
For doing the Halloween Hustle.

Skeleton shimmies, swings, and sways,
Be-bops as the music plays—
But Zombie's foot gets in the way . . .

Bones scatter!
What a clatter!
Spine is like a broken ladder!

A skeleton girl with a friendly smile
Sweeps the bones up in a pile.
"Skeleton, hey, in just a while,
You'll do the Halloween Hustle."

She uses a bottle of super-strong glue.
"You're fixed forever! You're just like new!
Hey, I'd like to dance with you!
Let's do the Halloween Hustle!"

All the monsters cheer and clap.
Bony thumbs and fingers snap.
Bony heels and toes tip-tap,
Doing the Halloween Hustle!